For my friends Cliff and Carisa!

First edition 2017

Library of Congress Catalog Card Number pending
ISBN 978-0-7636-8824-0

17 18 19 20 21 22 CCP 10 9 8 7 6 5 4 3 2 1

Printed in Shenzhen, Guangdong, China

FSC
www.fsc.org
MIX
Paper from
responsible sources
FSC® C008047

This book was typeset in Myriad.
The illustrations were done in ink, pencil, watercolor, and digital magic.

Candlewick Press
99 Dover Street
Somerville, Massachusetts 02144

visit us at www.candlewick.com

BOO WHO?

BEN CLANTON

CANDLEWICK PRESS

This is Boo.

Boo is new.

Being new can be scary,
even when everyone is friendly.

Boo has trouble fitting in.

He can't play bounce-ball.

Or pick-up twigs.

Or tag.

Would anyone even care
if Boo just disappeared?

BOO-HOO

Everyone else has started
a game of hide-and-seek.

Soon Gizmo finds Rex.

And Wild.

And Sprinkles.

But where is Boo?

Everyone helps look.

At last, a game that Boo can play!

This is Boo.
He's new, but he fits right in.

3...2...1...
READY OR NOT,
HERE I COME!

HEE-HEE!

BURP!

THIS IS MY SPOT!

SHHH!